For Owen,

whose laugh is one of the <u>best</u>
sounds in the world.

Illustrated by Keith Zarraga

Download coloring pages at mydadsbadjokes.com

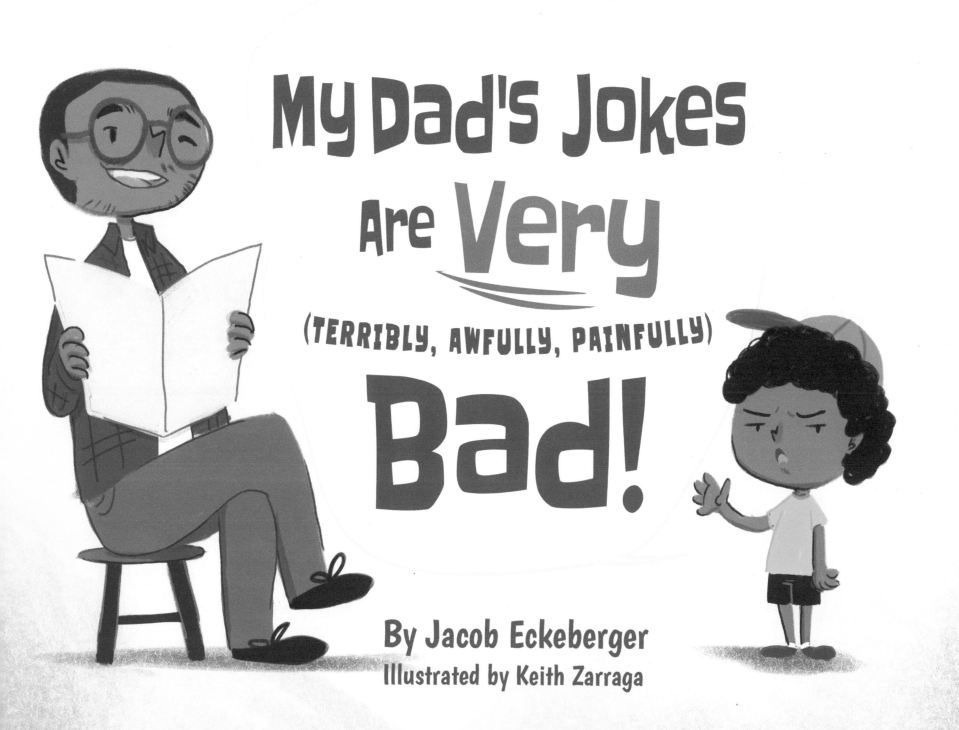

My Dad's Jokes Are Very

(TERRIBLY, AWFULLY, PAINFULLY)

Bad!

By Jacob Eckeberger

Illustrated by Keith Zarraga

Every day,
  it's always the same.
  You can see them
  coming from a mile away.

And I'm worried
nothing can stop this fad.
My Dad's jokes are very,
terribly, awfully, painfully bad.

See what I mean?
That's just the beginning.

Don't let him see you smile
Or you'll be here a while.

Remember,
you can't laugh one bit
Or he'll think
you're a fan of it.

No one should encourage him
Because it'll never end.

Our eye rolls don't seem to help.
And he doesn't even embarrass himself.

I think we should try to sneak away
Before he starts to make...

Let's try something this time.

When you see that glimmer in his eye
He's working on another joke to pitch.
And we'll act like we don't hear it.

Okay. Are you ready?
Let's hold steady...

How does the penguin build its house?

Igloos it together!

You're doing good. No laughing whatsoever.

Spring is here!

I'm so excited I might just wet my plants!

Wait! Don't crack now! This is our chance!

What's so bad about a nosey pepper?

It gets jalapeño business!

Don't smile or he'll keep up with this!

Well, we really did try.
There's just something
wrong with this guy.

I love him and he has lots of great qualities too. Maybe this is just a phase he's going through?

All i know
is that when I'm grown
My kids will definitely
be glad...

That their Dad's jokes aren't so very, terribly, awfully, painfully bad.